OISÍN McGANN

GET YOURSELF GONE

From the author
of Rat Runners

Also by Oisín McGann:
Books:
Rat Runners
Ancient Appetites
The Evil Eye
Strangled Silence
Series:
Armouron
The Forbidden Files
Mad Grandad

OISÍN McGANN

EDGE FRANKLIN WATTS

LONDON•SYDNEY

First published in 2013
by Franklin Watts

Text © Oisín McGann
Cover design by Peter Scoulding

Franklin Watts
338 Euston Road
London NW1 3BH

Franklin Watts Australia
Level 17/207 Kent Street
Sydney, NSW 2000

Picture credits: Alexander Yakovlev/
Shutterstock: front cover c.
kentoh/Shutterstock: front cover bl & cr.
peeterv/istockphoto: front cover bg.

pb ISBN: 978 1 4451 2312 7
eBook ISBN: 978 1 4451 2315 8
Library eBook ISBN : 978 1 4451 2577 0

1 3 5 7 9 10 8 6 4 2

Printed in Great Britain

Franklin Watts is a division of
Hachette Children's Books,
an Hachette UK company.
www.hachette.co.uk

For Jane, Anna, Moira and everyone involved in Poetry Ireland's hugely successful Writers in Schools Scheme.

Contents

Chapter One

I stand there, waiting to find out why I'm not dead yet. I should be dead. I'm standing in front of a crusty-looking, psycho Jamaican gangster by the name of Cyrus. One of the most powerful and dangerous men in the city.

Yesterday, I put his little brother, Brice, in hospital. It was sort of an accident.

"Vulgar Pluck," Cyrus rumbles.

He has old, intense, scary eyes. They look out at me through a curtain of thick dreadlocked hair that stretches down to his straggly beard.

"The boys found you at the train station, Vulgar," he growls at me. "Was you goin' somewhere?"

"Out of town," I reply, clearing my throat. "Way out of town."

That was my plan. After the fight with Brice, I sprinted home, packed a bag, and ran for the first train out of the city. I'd text my goodbyes once I was on the train. Then I'd keep going until I ran out of railway track. And then I'd change my name, dye my hair, try and grow a beard.

"You was too slow," Cyrus says simply.

"Yeah," I grunt.

There are five other people with us. We're standing in a building site. Work stopped here years ago and never started again. The other five are young — all about my age. They're Brice's friends, his crew. I've known them all since we were little kids. He calls them his Lost Boys, even though two of them are girls. They're the ones who caught me at the station. They didn't hurt me much. They were saving me for this — for Cyrus. They're watching me now with eyes like you'd see on a pack of jackals.

Cyrus wears layers of warm clothes and fingerless gloves. It's just after dawn, and he blows on his fingers in the chill air. I shiver, but it's not from the cold. It's a big building site and we're out of sight of the road. Out here, they can do anything to me.

"You hurt Brice," Cyrus says in a grating voice. "Sure, he started it — but he's my little bro. They operated on him last night — now

he's only got one nut. You shamed
him. I can't let that stand.
There's a reckoning to be had."

I should say something, but my
throat is tight with tension. Just
let it be quick whatever they're
going to do to me, I'm thinking.
That's all I ask, that it's quick.
Still, nothing happens, but I could
swear that the Lost Boys' eyes
start to glow. A cruel, toothy
smile spreads across Cyrus's face.
He stares at me and nods to
himself.

"We gonna give you a chance to get out of this, Vulgar my boy. Play a little game," he says.

I swallow, glance at the Lost Boys and their greedy stares. I wait.

"There's an old man on his way across town," Cyrus tells me. "He's carryin' a candle. The candle's lit. If the candle gets to where it's goin' it'll trigger dark magic — a spell of the most horrible kind. You got to stop that man. Blow out that candle before it gets where it's goin'. Do that for me, and I let this go."

I gaze at the ground, not sure what he's telling me.

"I have to catch this old man and blow out his candle?" I ask. "That's it?"

"Almost," Cyrus chuckles. "Brice's crew want to see you get your punishment, so they're goin' to come after you — try to stop you. You got a five-minute head-start. You got to blow out that candle before they get to you."

I'm up for this. Dark magic? Yeah, right. I've heard the rumours about Cyrus, of course. Blood sacrifices and talking to the dead. But I don't believe in all that rubbish. I'm pretty quick on my feet and I know this city. Let me get five minutes ahead of this pack of animals and I'll leave them in my dust. I nod to Cyrus.

He points out across the city. We're on a slight hill and in the dim, dirty yellow light of dawn, I can see a railway line far out to the west of us.

"The old man's on a train, on the Red Line," he says. "Heading north-east. He'll get off at Marlow Heights." His voice turns cold as the dawn. "If I was you, I'd get yourself gone."

So I do.

Chapter Two

I'm running hard across the rough,
broken ground of the building
site. I'm going all-out, my arms
and legs pumping, but I can't
keep this pace up for long. I just
want some distance between me
and the Lost Boys by the time I hit

the streets. Improves my chances of losing them.

I climb a weedy gravel bank and cross a road, then a railway line, but not the one I'm after. The old man is on a train that's cutting diagonally across town — coming from my left, out to a station way ahead of me. It has to make a lot of stops, but I still don't know if I can reach it in time.

The sounds of whoops and screeches carry through the clear, early morning air. Is that five

minutes already? The Lost Boys
are coming. Down the other side
of the bank, I leap over a wall and
find myself in an alley, stretching
behind a row of back gardens.
On instinct, I throw a glance
back over my shoulder towards
the railway tracks. A flicker of
movement catches my eye, but I
lose sight of it behind the wall.

That can't be them already.
Absolutely no way. Nobody's that
fast. My heart's going like crazy. I
remember the stories I've heard
about Cyrus's guys and what he

does to them sometimes, the
stuff he gives them. Stories of
bizarre manhunts through the city
at night. Invisible hunters, moving
like ghosts. It's all bull. And
nobody's that fast.

I flip myself over a chain-link
fence, and run across a backyard
littered with broken kids' toys,
a rusting swing-set and a slide.
Classy place. I head towards
the lane leading down the side
of a house. I hear the rattle of
someone coming over the fence
after me. I don't look back.

I dodge right, slam my foot into the kids' slide. It falls into the path of the Lost Boy and he trips over it. It's Marko, a small ginger whippet of a guy in a tracksuit. Quick as hell, but not too bright. He's scrambling up in an instant, the look of a savage on his face. But I've already grabbed a folded-up scooter that was lying on the ground. As he rolls up onto his feet, I smack it across the side of his head.

They make those scooters pretty solid. He drops like a sack of rocks. One down. I hear footsteps running down the alley at the back of the yard. I turn, heading out to the front of the house and the road beyond.

I'm in the suburbs — not my favourite type of place. I'm too visible in these open roads, the bland spread-out houses with their trim gardens and low walls. I need cluttered streets and corners to take cover. Angry shrieks reach out for me from somewhere behind.

I slow down as I cross the road.
I could follow it either way.
Instead, I bound straight ahead
and leap onto the wall in front of
me. It divides two front gardens,
and rises up to a wall at the back
going the same direction. This
wall is higher — taller than me. It
stretches down between two rows
of houses, with their back gardens
on either side of it.

This short cut will take me
between the houses to the main
road at the end. I can still move
pretty fast along the top of the

wall, but can't run all out, or I'd risk losing my balance. Still, it should slow them down too.

I don't know what makes me look back — some tiny noise or maybe just instinct. All I see is a blur of movement, hardly anything at all. I drop down flat on the wall and something — someone — lunges past over my head. Somebody trying a flying kick on me. On the top of the wall. Gutsy, flash even, but really stupid. I expect to see him fall sprawling off the side, but instead, two feet land lightly on the wall in front of me.

"Yo, Vulgar," a voice says. "Only thing getting snuffed out today is you."

His name's Frog. Could I really not see him before, or was it all just happening too fast? I jerk back and away as one of his feet kicks out at my head. The sole of an Adidas trainer brushes my nose. It stops and swings back and I just barely dodge it again.

Frog is lanky and loose with a frog

face and big flat frog hands and feet. He's a serious Taekwondo nut. He's good with it too. But he uses those flash kicks too much. Still can't figure out how he's staying up on the wall. I'm barely managing myself.

Frog's eyes have an unnatural glow in the gloomy light. He's as fast as a whip being cracked, but he places his feet perfectly. I duck under another powerful roundhouse kick, nearly lose my head doing it.

What the hell has Cyrus given them?

Chapter Three

Frog's jumping nimbly along the
top of the wall. But he loves
those high kicks. He swings at my
head again, and I swivel, spinning
in the same direction, my right
leg jabs out low as his goes high.
I take his foot out from under

him and he slips, drops...his balls crunch off the wall.

With a noise like a strangled gibbon, he topples sideways into the bushes below. You'd think Frog would've learned from Brice's mistake. Brice liked his high kicks too. He's in hospital because I caught his foot, but fell backwards, still holding onto it. That's how it happened — I fell. It was an accident. It wasn't my fault I was standing in front of a concrete bollard. I hit the ground and Brice fell on the bollard.

Doing the splits. He should've
kept his fancy kicks to himself.

So anyway, two Lost Boys down.
I cast a look behind me, but can't
see anyone else. They've gone
quiet, but that doesn't make me
feel any better. That's twice I've
been held up. Two chances for the
others to catch up.

I reach the end of the wall
without running into anyone
else. There's another suburban
estate on the far side of the
road. I'm moving fast again,

leaping low walls, climbing higher ones, keeping to cover where I can. Further on, I'm getting into narrower streets, higher buildings. My kind of environment.

Turning into a narrow alley, I slow down, trying to catch my breath. Need to pace myself a bit. Heart's going like a machine gun. My leg muscles are burning, but they'll ease off if I keep moving at a steadier rate.

Something flashes past overhead,

crossing from the roof on one side of the alley to the other. They're on the roofs? I'm so busy looking up, I almost miss the little minx who's suddenly standing right in front of me. Her name's Star. I raise my hands, but she has hers up first. She blows some kind of powder into my face, like she's blowing me a kiss.

I blink and cough, a burning pain in my nose and throat. Everything tilts and sways. There was something weird in that powder. For a moment, Star looks like she's on fire.

She still looks good. She's hot in a kind of really outdated bad girl kind of way. Punk-pink spikes in her hair. A studded leather jacket and trousers that were just the coolest thing in the 1980s. There are teardrops tattooed on her left cheek.

The evil cow punches me right on the nose and my world spins. The flames coming off her don't burn, so that's just me seeing things. I'm pretty sure those wheelie-bins

don't have teeth either. The
buildings judder around me.
The punches are real though —
pain stabs through the sickening
visions. I turn and run, but my
legs feel like liquorice.

"You go, boy!" Star laughs. "You
really think we're gonna let you
get that candle before it gets
you?"

She kicks me up the ass. It helps.
I start running properly. Not
so fast that I've any chance of
escaping, but fast enough to make

her run after me. The narrow
alley pitches and rolls like a ship.

Up to my right, I see a man in a
window at my head-height. He's
soaping up his face for a shave.
I slap the window as I run past,
making him jump. Star's calling
after me, cackling, sprinting to
catch up. The man's furious. He
shoves the window right open.
The edge of the frame slams into
Star's face, her head snaps back
and her legs crumple under her.
She's not unconscious, but she's
completely stunned, clutching her

head and moaning. Three down.
The man roars curses at us.

I run.

Above me, roof tiles shift and
click under somebody's feet. I
keep moving, but Star's words
are scratching at my brain now:
"Think we're gonna let you get
that candle before it gets you?"

Just what the hell is that candle
meant to do?

Chapter Four

Vision's all screwed up. Can't think. Gotta get my head straight. Not even sure I'm going in the right direction. I stagger out into a street, nearly running into the pole of a Stop sign. I hang on to it and look around. The street's empty. Parked cars and a couple of motorbikes. No people, not even a taxi. The sun's still low, so the whole place is in shadow. There's a railway bridge at the end of the street to my left. That's the Red Line. Fear creeps under my skin.

The station's still a few hundred metres from here. Have I missed the train? The thought has barely passed through my head when someone lands behind me. The one who was following across the roofs. I swing round the pole so it's between me and the girl named Surf.

She's in tracksuit bottoms and a pink belly top. Long, blonde dreadlocks hang down over her shoulders. Her face is a narrow, pinched scowl. Surf's a surfer girl, but that's where the happy image ends. She's also a raving nutter.

"Slow and weak," she sneers. "That's always been your problem."

"Can we make this quick?" I snap

at her. "I've got a train to catch."

She pulls a bicycle chain from around her waist and starts swinging it. I duck right and left, avoiding each strike by keeping the pole between us. My head's spinning. The chain smacks the pole, then flies round to come at me from the other side. I pull back and it wraps around the pole again. I grab it, take a hold further up and yank it.

Surf stumbles forward, and I seize her hair and whack her head off the pole. She cries out, and goes to pull away. I get two handfuls of hair and wrench them either side of the pole. I tie them in a good tight knot and step back.

She's tied to the Stop sign by her own hair. I search her quickly to make sure she doesn't have a knife to cut herself free. Then I run on. Four down — and the fifth one is the slowest of the bunch. I could still leave him behind. My head's getting clearer. I run as fast as I ever have. I can hear the sound of a train ahead of me.

Chapter Five

A couple of minutes later, I
reach Marlow Heights Station.
The train's pulling away. I look
desperately about, the breaths
heaving into my chest. I've missed
him. I've missed him. Then...

there — past the bridge, walking
down the street. Heading towards
my street. The street I live on.
An old wispy-haired Oriental
man carrying a candle in a little
narrow glass. I don't believe in
dark magic, but suddenly I'm
terrified of that man and his
candle.

As I sprint under the bridge,
a section of shadow moves. A
large figure sticks out his arm
to clothesline me. It catches
me across the throat and drops
me flat on my back. He was just

standing back against the wall.
How did I not see him?

"Too slow, my man! You're gonna
burn!"

His name is Keefer, and he's
Brice's best friend. A lean,
pale, bleached-blond guy with a
widow's peak and the face of a
vampire. He kicks me in the head
with steel-capped boots sending
bursts of sparks through my skull,
then pulls out a long, cruel-
looking knife.

"Let's see how much I can do to you," he says. "Before Cyrus's curse cooks you."

I'm trying to get my senses back online, but my reflexes are still up for it. I manage to grab his foot and kick him in the stomach. He stumbles back. His boot comes off in my hands. He's not wearing socks. I'm still groggy, but I'm on my feet before he comes at me again. I block the knife with his boot once, twice, three times. He's getting frustrated, cursing, jabbing and swinging violently.

I knock the blade away one more time, then stamp on his bare foot. He lets out a yell. As he's distracted, I drive the sole of his own boot into his face. I pull it back to see an astonished expression on his face. I hit him again and he topples backward. Five down.

I run.

The old man's nearly at my house. Of course he was going there the whole time — of course the candle was meant for me.

That's the twisted way Cyrus's mind works. The Oriental guy is bending to place the glass on my doorstep. I grab the glass with one hand and shove him aside with the other. There's a thin layer of wax left on the bottom of the glass. The flame is starting to sputter as it runs out of wick.

I'm about to blow it out, when I stop. What if it's a trick? What if they want me to blow out the candle? What if that was the plan the whole time? The flame is flickering weakly. No, the Lost

Boys were serious. They wanted to stop me. They wanted revenge.

I put my mouth to the top of the glass and blow out the dying flame.

The old man is still lying on the ground beside me from when I pushed him. He grunts and picks himself up slowly, brushing himself down. Then he eyes me up. I'm sure one of those eyes is glass.

"What would have happened?"

I ask him. "If the flame burned out before I got here?"

The man snorts and stares at me coldly.

"But it didn't, did it?" he replies. "Just leave it at that, boy... and be glad."

And then he walks away, leaving me holding the dead candle.

About the author

Oisín McGann has written and illustrated over 25 books. He'll probably keep doing it unless somebody stops him. He was born and raised in Ireland, so he got off to a bad start. Then he went to art college, where he failed to learn anything useful.

When he left college, Oisín realised he'd probably never get a proper job — which made him very happy indeed. So he worked as a freelance artist for a while, drawing and painting for money. He painted on everything from cars to walls, from jackets to bike helmets.

This racket went on for a few years. Then, for reasons we won't talk about, he left Ireland in a hurry, and found his way to London. He figured nobody trusted him anyway, so he got a job with an advertising company. Working as a copy writer and art director, he spent his time making up weird ways of selling things. It was excellent training for writing fiction.

He wrote so many dodgy ads,
the English asked the Irish to
take him back.

Oisín now lives somewhere in the
Irish countryside, where he hopes
people cannot find him. He's still
writing and illustrating, and he
can't believe he's still getting
away with it. If you should see
him, do not approach him, as he
may be rude. If you like this
story, you can dig up more
about Oisín and his work at
www.oisinmcgann.com.

WILLIAM HUSSEY

THE NIGHTMARE EATER

FROM THE AUTHOR OF WITCHFINDER

EDGE RIVETS

If you enjoyed reading *Get Yourself Gone*, you might also like *The Nightmare Eater* by William Hussey.

Imagine your very worst fear.
The kind of fear that visits
you in the middle of the night and
leaves you gasping for breath. The kind
of fear you keep buried deep, deep down.

Tomasz Kaczmarek knows all about that
kind of fear. And he's about to find out
what happens when your very worst fears
come true...

Buy online at
www.franklinwatts.co.uk.
978 1 4451 2311 0 paperback
978 1 4451 2314 1 eBook

Turn over to read an extract from
The Nightmare Eater.

Tomasz found himself trapped in a windowless chamber about the size of a basketball court. Overhead, a single bulb struggled against the dusty darkness. He was still recovering from the wall's deafening *clang* when Balfus' voice echoed around the room.

"Please remain calm. This is all part of the horror house experience. Please remain calm. This is..." The message continued on a recorded loop. Weirdest. Fairground. Attraction. Ever! The falling wall had shocked him all right, but this empty room hardly qualified as the scariest horror house in the world...

Something shifted: a figure rising out of the gloom on the far side of the chamber. While Balfus' message bounced from wall to wall, the small, stooped shape gathered substance, like a nightmare willing itself into reality. It started tottering towards him and Tomasz backed up against the metal wall.

Bowling ahead of the figure came an aroma of rotting vegetation, mixed in with the metallic tang of old blood. The kind of scent he had always associated with the witch Baba Jaga from his grandpa's stories.

"Are you there?" asked a reedy voice. "The moon is full and I want you to come to my chicken-leg house…"

Feature by feature, she emerged from the shadows: first, the crook nose with its festering sores; then a nest of bone-white hair laced with autumn leaves; twisted hands like eagles' talons; eyes the colour of burning embers; and finally, thin black lips smeared with the blood of a thousand children.

"Come now, it's almost suppertime."

Want to find out what happens in the grisly House of Horrors? Get your hands on a copy of *The Nightmare Eater* today!

More from the **RIVETS** series

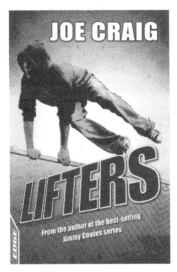

978 1 4451 0555 0 pb
978 1 4451 0850 6 eBook

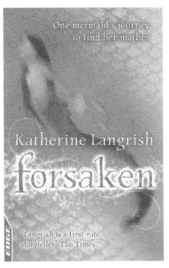

978 1 4451 0557 4 pb
978 1 4451 1073 8 eBook

978 1 4451 0556 7 pb
978 1 4451 0849 0 eBook

978 1 4451 0707 3 pb
978 1 4451 1072 1 eBook